MY BROTHER IS A ROBOT

ROBOT

BOOK 3

THE SWITCH

AMANDA RONAN

The Switch
My Brother is a Robot #3

Copyright © 2016

Published by Scobre Educational

Written by Amanda Ronan

Printed in the United States of America.

Scobre Educational
2255 Calle Clara
La Jolla, CA 92037

Scobre Operations & Administration
42982 Osgood Road
Fremont, CA 94539

www.scobre.com
info@scobre.com

Scobre Educational publications may be purchased for educational, business, or sales promotional use.

Cover and layout design by Nicole Ramsay
Copyedited by Kristin Russo

ISBN: 978-1-62920-501-4 (Library Bound)
ISBN: 978-1-62920-500-7 (eBook)

For Jack.

Being your tía is the best job in the world.

CHAPTER 1

"**K**EEP YOUR BLINDFOLDS ON, SHAWN. NO PEEKING," Cyrus laughed as he led my mom and me into the kitchen.

"I wasn't peeking," I said, lowering my hand away from the scarf around my face.

"Cyrus, I can't wait to see what you and your father have been working on!" My mom had been excited during the whole project, both that we were getting a new kitchen and that Dad and Cyrus were spending so much time together.

"Okay, take a look!" Cyrus announced after leading us through the door from the living room to the kitchen.

I pulled off my blindfold and took a look around. The new kitchen was impressive—a six-burner stovetop, a double oven, a state-of-the-art refrigerator, new cabinets, new tile on the walls and floor, and, most importantly, a new water bowl and dog bed for Scooter, my favorite basset hound. "Whoa," I whispered, "very cool."

My mom looked around with pride. "This is so beautiful. You two did such a great job."

My dad nudged Cyrus a little. "It never would have happened without my boy, here."

Cyrus grinned like a goofball. "Thanks, Dad."

It had been a month since my brother Cyrus had tried to renovate the kitchen by himself as a surprise for my dad. You might think it sounds a little strange that a kid tried renovating a kitchen, but Cyrus isn't exactly a kid; he's actually a robot with an amazing super-computer mind. My mom is a mechanical engineer, and Cyrus is her project. He's lived with us for about three months and it's been an interesting journey so far. See, the other strange thing about Cyrus, besides being a robot, is that he happens to look just like me. My mom forgot to design the outside of the robot, so the artists at the lab used my picture to create Cyrus.

He was far from perfect when he first moved in. His alarms would go off in the middle of the night, and he didn't know how to feel the same emotions that humans do, so he'd scream at babies and laugh at cockroaches. He even helped me cheat on my homework, which got me kicked off the basketball team. My dad, who likes rules and structure, did not like all the disruptions Cyrus brought with him. But since Cyrus took the time to get to know my dad, the two of them have been really close. They spent the last month rebuilding the kitchen together. Now you'd never know that Cyrus wasn't actually my dad's son. I was jealous of Cyrus at first, but now I think having him around is really fun. I finally got the brother I'd always wanted; he just happened to be a twin brother.

"So, Shawn, do you want to see what your brother added into the kitchen designs just for you?" my dad asked, pointing near the new sink.

My eyed widened. "Yeah!" My mind raced. I had asked Cyrus to include a soda fountain, a frozen yogurt dispenser, or a popcorn machine. I wondered which I was getting.

My dad opened a cabinet door and revealed . . . a dishwasher. "Ta-da! It should fit the whole family's dishes!"

My face fell. Really? A dishwasher? "Oh."

"It'll make your chores go faster at night. There's no prewashing, you just have to load it!" Cyrus exclaimed moving closer to the dishwasher. "And it's environmentally friendly. I rebuilt it so the water cycles for reuse."

My dad patted Cyrus on the back again and added, "In fact, the whole kitchen is eco-friendly. It's got low VOC paint, the cabinets are made from reclaimed wood, the tile is actually recycled glass, and the flooring is made from recycled water bottles."

I didn't even know what low VOC paint was but I couldn't care less. After all the work I'd done to help Cyrus plan this thing and all I got was a dishwasher. I was ready to stop celebrating the new kitchen. "Can I go to my room? I want to get to bed early. Coach might let me play tomorrow."

I had started going to after-school tutoring three days a week to help me bring up my grades in math. My math teacher, who was also my basketball coach, noticed my effort and finally let me rejoin the team last week. I wasn't allowed to play against other teams yet, but I could go to practice and sit on the bench during games.

Dad smiled and waved me out of the room. "Go on to bed." He turned to Cyrus. "You too. You deserve to turn in early after all your hard work."

Cyrus walked into the living room with me. He usually slept in my mom's office. "Hey, Shawn?"

I turned and looked at him. "Hmm?"

Cyrus leaned forward and lowered his voice, "There's a hidden vending machine behind the pots and pans. I stocked it with your favorite candy bar, and I rewired it so it's free. Just type *1 2 3 4* on the keypad."

"Seriously?" I asked as my mouth salivated. The thought of crispy rice and caramel bars covered in milk chocolate just sitting around and not being eaten made me eager to have another look around the kitchen.

Cyrus nodded. "Yep. I thought you might want something more than a dishwasher, so I improvised.

We have to keep it hidden, though. You know how Dad feels about junk food." He held out his hand and we did our secret handshake.

"You're the best brother ever!" I laughed and went upstairs, plotting my return to the kitchen once my parents went to bed.

"Can you believe that math project? I'm never going to finish it in time," I groaned to my best friend James as we walked to lunch.

"You have all weekend. Come to practice, play the game, and then work on it Saturday night and all day Sunday," he said. He slapped my back encouragingly and then went to stand in line for lunch. I tossed my lunch bag on the table where I always sat with the other guys from the team.

"What is that?" Jensen asked and pointed to my lunch as I pulled out deviled eggs, gray mush on bread, a fruit salad, and a thermos of homemade almond milk. "Where's your sandwich?"

I rolled my eyes. "Dad and Cyrus finished the kitchen. We've been eating all kinds of weird, gourmet foods." Cyrus sat down across from me. I held up the gray thing and asked, "What's in this?"

"It's a locally sourced eggplant, with heirloom tomatoes, and roasted garlic, on slices of a dried out, homemade baguette," Cyrus smiled. He'd really gotten into cooking with our dad. Of course, Cyrus couldn't actually eat food, so his enthusiasm was all about making the food and not actually tasting it.

I sighed and looked around. "Maybe someone will trade. I'd kill for a snack cake." I saw a few kids watching Cyrus. He was still a minor celebrity in the halls. Lots of people in the community were not supportive about him being at school. They had threatened to pull their kids out if Cyrus continued to attend classes, but none of them actually had. Cyrus was hardly a threat to anyone, except maybe me with this gross food.

I was feeling antsy about the project, so I popped half of a deviled egg in my mouth and asked, "Wanna go to the gym and shoot some hoops, Cyrus?"

He nodded.

I wrapped up the rest of my lunch and held out my thermos. "Almond milk, anyone?"

The guys snorted and waved me away with a few dismissive hands.

CHAPTER 2

WHEN WE GOT TO THE GYM, COACH VELAZQUEZ WAS IN there with a couple of the new starters on the team. I bounced the ball a few times and was about to take a shot when Cyrus jumped in front of me, knocked the ball out of my hands and made a layup. He did a little victory dance, which was something he'd picked up watching James and me play on the street by our house.

"Very nice, Cyrus!" Coach called and jogged over to where I was still standing. "Focus, Shawn. You'll get back in the game soon. In the meantime, it's nice to see you putting in the extra practice at lunch."

Cyrus rebounded the ball and tossed it to me. I nodded at Coach. "I'll keep working on it." He patted me on the back and went back to work with Billy, one of the new starters. I stopped dribbling and watched them practice for a few minutes. Billy wasn't a confident player. He hesitated and questioned his next moves.

Cyrus noticed the same thing and whispered, "Looks like you might be back in the game sooner than Coach thought. He's nowhere near as good as you."

I smiled and shrugged, trying to play off Cyrus's compliment. But the truth was, he was right. We played one-on-one for the next few minutes and I nailed every shot I went for.

When the bell ran, Cyrus and I put the ball back on the rack. When we got to the gym door, Coach

Velasquez called out, "Hey, Shawn, be ready to play tomorrow."

"I will!" I smiled.

Cyrus punched my arm lightly and said in his best announcer's voice, "And . . . he's back!"

"Cyrus!" I yelled from my room in a panic the next morning. I looked at the clock and started tapping my feet nervously.

Cyrus stuck his head through my door and asked, "What's up?"

"Come in." I waved and whispered, "Shut the door behind you."

Cyrus swung the door closed and sat on my bed. "What's wrong?"

"Have you done the math project yet?" I pointed at what was supposed to be a three-dimentional model of a town but looked more like an underwater scene made from torn paper and tape.

Cyrus looked closer at my project. "Is that supposed to be . . . " He flicked a piece of paper that was flopping over on its side. "Why didn't you use something sturdy to build the town? None of your shapes look like polygons and there are no right angles because everything is so . . . "

"Horrible?" I asked.

"Not great," Cyrus agreed. "I made mine out of left over kitchen remodel materials. There's probably enough for you to use, too."

I shook my head. "I won't have time to start over. I have to go to practice and then the game is right after." I sighed. I could not blow this chance to get back on the team. But I had to finish this project or I'd be kicked off the team again, anyway.

"Well," Cyrus looked around. "I could help you with your project."

"No way!" I shook my head. "The last time you helped me with my math work, I got kicked off the team for cheating. I need to do this myself." I bit my lip. "But there might be something else you could do."

Cyrus closed his eyes and started calculating the possibilities of what I was going to ask him, "You want me to pretend to be you at practice and at the game."

I nodded eagerly, "Yes! I just need a few hours to make this project better. Then I'll bike over to school and we can switch back. Will you?" I got out of my chair and dragged Cyrus to the full-length mirror on my closet. Even standing side-by-side we looked exactly alike. My mom had designed Cyrus to be as life-like as possible. He moved just like a human, without a trace of jerky, robotic movements. "This could work."

Cyrus watched us in the mirror and finally nodded. "On one condition, no one can find out," he said.

I shrugged. "Sure. No big deal."

"I mean it, Shawn. No one can know." Cyrus's face had gone very serious.

"What's the big deal?" I laughed, thinking he was making this more dramatic than it had to be.

"Some of the other engineers at Smith and Company have kids on the opposing team. They'll be in the crowd watching the game today. They can't know I was pretending to be you." Cyrus's seriousness made sense once he explained. Part of the backlash about Cyrus acting like a student came from some of other engineers at my mom's work. They were jealous of her success and tried to make her look bad when the news of Cyrus first broke. Smith and Company Lab stood behind her, but in their press release, they assured people that Cyrus wasn't trying to become a human or take over human bodies in any supernatural sort of way. If they found out that Cyrus was impersonating me, we'd get in big trouble with Mom's bosses.

"It's a big risk," I sighed. "Never mind. I think we should forget it. I'll just call Coach and explain that

I need to do my project. He'll probably be cool with that."

My dad stepped into my room right then and said, "Hey, boys. Excited for the game?" He was wearing Chavez Elementary School colors and had duct taped my number to the back of his t-shirt.

"Go, team!" Cyrus smiled and waved his fists.

"Proud of you, Shawn. It'll be good to see you on the court again." My dad gave me a little salute and then left the room.

I sighed, "This is not good."

Cyrus stood up. "It's fine. I'm going in your place. Email me when you're leaving the house and I'll fake an injury. Meet me in the locker room."

"Seriously, you think this will work?" I asked.

Cyrus smiled. "Of course it will. What could go wrong?"

CHAPTER 3

THREE HOURS LATER, I PULLED MY HOOD TIGHTLY AROUND my head and kept my eyes on the floor as I snuck into the gym. The game was just a few seconds away from half-time when I heard a whistle and a ref call, "Foul on the Colts. Cole, take your place at the free throw line."

I looked up and saw Cyrus dribble confidently, his toes close to the line. He looked up at the net, raised his arms and took his first shot. *Swish.* The ball didn't even hit the rim. I could hear my dad cheering in the stands.

Cyrus made his second shot, too. He was making me look good out there.

When I turned to head into the locker room, I bumped into someone tall. As I backed away to look up at his face I could feel a knot forming in my stomach. It was Dr. Geno, from Mom's lab. He was one of the loudest opponents of Cyrus's integration into the community. His son was on the Colts' team. This was exactly the kind of exposure we were trying to avoid. I swallowed and hoped I could pull off a good Cyrus impression.

"Well hello, CY-159." Dr. Geno smiled. He refused to call Cyrus by his name in press conferences, instead always referring to him by his lab code.

"Hello, Dr. Geno," I said with as little emotion as possible. Cyrus didn't like this guy; I knew that from watching the news with him. He said Dr. Geno was a sorry excuse for a scientist because he was trying to stop Mom's research rather than help it along.

Dr. Geno tilted his head to one side. "Hmm . . . " He leaned down a little and his face got closer to mine, "Did you have some recent remodeling done?"

I took a step back to get him out of my personal space. "No."

"Because I don't remember the lab giving you pimply skin." He pointed to the side of my face where I had a few breakouts.

What a jerk, I thought to myself. "We're just trying to be as realistic as possible," I said aloud.

"Yes," Dr. Geno replied. "Turn around so I can check your data log. I want to commend the artist who worked on you for their accurate and precise work. It's just remarkable how real that acne looks."

I gulped. Dr. Geno wasn't going to find a fold out keyboard tucked away in my neck. When the buzzer went off announcing the end of the half, I hoped the rush of players to the locker rooms would separate the two of us. Instead, I felt a hand clap on my shoulder,

"Cyrus! You changed your mind!" At home, I had pretended to be Cyrus and pretended to have work to do to avoid having to go to the game. So my dad was surprised to see me—er, Cyrus.

"Nathaniel Cole," my dad introduced himself to Dr. Geno, even though already he knew exactly who the scientist was. Dad had watched the news with great interest when Cyrus first came to stay.

"Richard Geno, I work with your wife at Smith and Company." Dr. Geno shook my dad's hand confidently.

"Yes, so you know Cyrus, here." Dad put his arm around my shoulder.

Dr. Geno cleared his throat. "Actually, that's not Cyrus. That's your son, Shawn." He pointed to Cyrus who was jogging by with the rest of the team. "That's Cyrus, or rather CY-159."

"Shawn?" Dad looked closely at me and suddenly realized what was going on. "What have you boys done?"

The weekend continued to get worse. On Sunday night we sat together in the living room and watched Dr. Geno on the local news channel. He showed video of Cyrus excelling in the basketball game.

"So, Dr. Geno, explain to our viewers why this is so terrible. I mean, it looks harmless. It's just a boy playing basketball." The newscaster smiled at the camera.

Dr. Geno raised an eyebrow menacingly and said, "I wish I could tell you that this was just a harmless boy, but, actually, Bob, it's a robot built at Smith and Company Labs. He pretended to act as a human in this game. Impersonating a human is serious, especially when this robot has mental and physical capabilities that far outweigh our own."

Bob chuckled nervously and cleared his throat before asking, "So what you're saying is that this is the robot Smith and Company Labs promised us was harmless, but now you think he could be dangerous?"

Dr. Geno nodded. "I know that's not what anybody wanted to hear, because this robot is going to school and acting like a real boy. But he has the potential to be a real threat. Imagine if there were more like him. They could engage in dangerous, even illegal activities, all while pretending to be human. We need to—"

"Enough of this garbage." My dad turned off the television.

"But Dad, what are we going to do about what Dr. Geno's saying? It's not true. Cyrus isn't dangerous," I said, looking for a plan.

My mom sighed heavily. She would fight for Cyrus and for her project. "You won't do anything, Shawn. Let your dad and me handle this, okay?"

I could tell by her tone that the issue wasn't up for discussion any longer. I mumbled an agreement but started formulating a plan as soon as I got to my room.

I texted some of the guys from the team, *Meet me in the gym @ lunch tmrw.*

"I don't know, Shawn. My mom told me to stay away from Cyrus. She's worried he'll go all crazy robot on me," said Colton, a point guard on the team.

James laughed, "Come on. That's stupid. We all know how awesome Cyrus is. Nothing bad is going to happen." James had been my best friend since we were babies. We'd lived three houses away from each other our whole lives. I knew he'd do whatever he could to help.

Jensen shrugged. "I'm in. I like Cyrus. He's a little weird, but he's cool. And my mom said to stay away from him, too, which makes me want to do this even more."

I laughed and looked at Demarcus. "What about you?"

He nodded. Demarcus was new to the team this year and was still a little shy. "I'll help."

"Fine," Colton groaned. "Me too."

"The plan is to start going crazy on social media, sharing all the great things Cyrus does. You can make stuff up if you need to. Basically, send messages, post pictures, share videos, do whatever you have to do to get people talking about Cyrus. If we can show everyone we know how great he is, and they show everyone they know . . . well, then a lot of people will see that Cyrus isn't dangerous and that my mom's project shouldn't be shut down," I explained.

James thought for a minute. "Since Cyrus isn't allowed at school right now, you should all come over after school and Shawn can bring Cyrus. We can start then."

Everyone agreed and by the end of lunch, I was sure our plan would work. If a cat that frowned and a dog that looked like a teddy bear could become Internet sensations, surely, with our help, Cyrus could become one, too.

CHAPTER 4

"**Y**OU WANT ME TO DO *WHAT* WITH THIS CAT?" CYRUS asked, looking at James's pet kitten, Flip-flop.

I pointed to the big oak tree and said, "Climb up that tree and pretend to be rescuing the cat. We're all going to take pictures and post them online." Colton, Demarcus, James, and Jensen were waiting with their phones.

"Shawn, this is ridiculous," Cyrus started to protest.

"Just do it. We're going to save your reputation. You'll see." I shoved Cyrus toward the tree and watched him climb, Flip-flop hidden safely in his shirt pocket.

Once we got the shot, each of us captioned it and sent it to our friends in social media. I captioned my picture, *My brother Cy saving a kitten. Couldn't be more proud!*

"What's next?" asked Colton. He was finally getting into the spirit.

James pointed to the house. "The kitchen. Cyrus can pull cans from the pantry for the local food bank."

Jensen laughed, "Oh, that's good!"

Cyrus rolled his eyes but stayed silent as he followed us into the house. He posed with stacks of canned vegetables. Demarcus got fifteen likes in the first minute of posting his picture with the caption: *Cyrus thinks there's nothing corn-y about helping the community.*

After we put the cans away we went to the front lawn. Colton suggested we take photos of Cyrus like he was mowing the lawn of our elderly neighbor, Mr. Graham. Cyrus knocked on Mr. Graham's door to get permission to be in his yard.

"So, you're saying you want to pretend to mow my lawn? I'll tell you what, boy, you really mow my lawn and you can take your pictures." Mr. Graham smiled, looking very pleased with himself.

"Sure," Cyrus agreed. While he pushed the mower back and forth in Mr. Graham's yard, Demarcus, Jensen, Colton and I took pictures, made new memes, and started watching the comments come in. By the time he was done mowing the lawn, *#CyrustheGreat* was trending.

"I feel like we need one more big thing to show that Cyrus can be really helpful," Jensen said while James and Cyrus put the lawn mower away in the garage.

Demarcus agreed. "Yeah, like something that shows he can help people in ways other humans can't."

They both had a point. So far we'd shown Cyrus

doing things that normal humans do every day. What we needed was a job for a robot.

"Shawn, I've gone along with your silly plan all day, but this is ridiculous. I was designed to help people." Cyrus crossed his arms in front of his chest and refused to come inside the store.

I looked over his shoulder at the crowd of girls lined up and said, "This *is* helping people. Trust me. You're helping Mrs. McClure, you're helping the girls, and you're helping me."

"How is this helping you?" Cyrus raised an eyebrow. He didn't like this latest plan one bit.

"Well, if this works, you'll stay. I'd miss you if you had to leave, bro." I smiled at Cyrus, but watched Chantal Baxter laugh with her friends behind him.

Cyrus turned around and chuckled. "You mean, if this works, all these girls will think you're soooo cool."

I laughed. "Well, yeah, that too."

Cyrus shook his head and said, "Fine, let's get this over with."

James's mom, Mrs. McClure, owned a trendy girls clothing store in the middle of town. Before heading over there, the guys and I had messaged everyone we knew to come down to *She-She*. The plan was that Cyrus would be a fashion stylist for the day, giving advice to the girls about what would look good on them. He'd be able to run statistics on certain outfits and let girls know how many times they'd wear it, if their parents would approve, and how cute they'd look compared to other girls in the same outfit.

Mrs. McClure wrapped her arm around Cyrus and said, "Thank you for doing this, Cy. This is really going to help business. You ready to get started?"

Cyrus looked at me like I was crazy and nodded his head. While Mrs. McClure explained to the girls how the styling would work, Cyrus sat on a stool and waited.

The first girl to approach him was Bethany Dodge. She stood in front of the wall while Cyrus took pictures with the cameras in his eyeballs. He held out the tablet built in his palm for her to see the outfits he'd picked out for her. "Basically, I'd avoid anything in red, if I were you. It doesn't go with your complexion," Cyrus told her. Bethany squealed with delight and went with Mrs. McClure to go find the skirt Cyrus had just recommended.

"Her complexion? How do you even know about that stuff?" I laughed and asked Cyrus as the next girl got ready to pose.

Cyrus tapped his forehead. "The curse of instant downloads. I know everything, Shawn. Yet, I don't know how you suckered me into this."

The next hour was truly hysterical. Cyrus eventually started loosening up and having a good time. His advice was right on and a lot of girls left with a few outfits that made them look really good. After word got out about what Cyrus was doing, the moms who brought the girls to the shop started getting into the styling. Soon Cyrus was giving advice about pleats and plaid, stripes and wearing white after Labor Day.

When it was Chantal's turn, Cyrus ran his scan and showed her the results. "Basically, you'll look good in anything."

She giggled. "That's sweet."

Cyrus scratched his head and said, "No, that wasn't a compliment. It's statistically true."

"Oh well, it was still sweet." Chantal smiled and walked over to her friends. After a second of talking, they all squealed and looked over at Cyrus.

"I think they like you, man," I whispered to a confused-looking Cyrus.

He shrugged and said, "Well, the data doesn't lie." Then he turned back to Mrs. Holt and said, "I think a sensible navy blue heel will look the best with the pinstriped trousers."

Dr. Geno did not appreciate our social media campaign to save Cyrus. The next night, he held another press conference, but this time he invited Dr. Smith, the founder and CEO of Smith and Company Lab.

"These antics should not be tolerated," Dr. Geno said looking directly into the camera. "The photos and videos that are being passed around the community are hoaxes. They were carefully designed to make CY-159 look like a contributing member of the community. I have with me today Dr. Smith, who oversees everything at Smith and Company Lab, who has some very interesting things to say."

Dr. Geno stepped away from the microphone to let Dr. Smith speak. His forehead was creased in thought and he rubbed his temples before speaking. "When the prototypes for human-like robots were first being developed at our lab, we envisioned machines that would save time, save money, and possibly save lives. We did not design multi-million dollar robots to become fashionistas. It is with great disappointment that we are considering suspending the robotics program at Smith and Company Lab indefinitely. There will be a community meeting to discuss the decision later this week. Thank you and goodnight."

CHAPTER 5

"**P**ROMISE ME NO MORE STUFF ON THE INTERNET," CYRUS pleaded with me before I left to go to school the next morning. "The lab thought it was a joke, and now Mom's job is in jeopardy. *Please*, don't do anything else."

I shrugged and said, "Fine. But I was just trying to help, you know. You could be a little more grateful."

Cyrus sighed, "Shawn, I am thankful you wanted to help, you know that. But this isn't what was supposed to happen."

I nodded. "I get it. I'll quit the campaign." I turned to walk down the driveway, but looked back and asked, "You're still coming to dinner with the team after the game tonight, right?"

"I wouldn't miss it," Cyrus said before turning to go back in the house.

At school, a bunch of girls came up to me asking about Cyrus. They were all excited to show him how their new outfits looked. I can't say I missed him too much when I had to tell them, "Sorry, he still can't come to school, but you can show me!"

Other kids that I had never even talked to said nice things about Cyrus to me while I was walking down the halls. They showed me their favorite pictures and told me how many times they liked and favorited our videos. The social media stuff might not have worked on the lab, but it definitely got a crowd of kids to support Cyrus.

Even guys on the opposing team asked about Cyrus

at the game. They scanned the crowd looking for him. One of them asked if I thought Cyrus would sign the game ball for him. Cyrus didn't come to the game, but it was clear that many people who came to watch were there to see him.

"Aw, Cyrus man, you should have been there. I made a layup like a pro!" Jensen laughed with his mouth full of pizza, reliving his game winning basket.

Cyrus tilted his head to one side and said, "Please don't talk with your mouth full. It's disgusting."

"Cyrus," I laughed, "that's rude."

"No," Cyrus shook his head, "It's rude to show a table full of people your partially chewed food."

"Okay." I grabbed Cyrus's arm and dragged him over to the skee-ball area in the arcade section of the pizza place. "What's with you? Ever since you got here, you've been a jerk."

Cyrus sighed and closed his eyes. "I've spent all

day running possibilities and it doesn't look good. My project is definitely going to end. There's no way around it."

"Come on, man, that can't be true. Mom will find some way to keep it going," I tried reassuring him.

"That's the biggest problem. Mom had me start running shut down protocols. I've been saving and backing up data all day. I'm stressed and a little sad, I think."

"You think?" I laughed.

He nodded. "It's an unusual feeling, one that's coming from somewhere other than my databases."

"You are such a weird guy. What am I going to do without you?" I bit my lip and tried not to get emotional.

"Shawn?" Cyrus asked, looking over my shoulder.

I waved him away, "No . . . I'm okay. You don't have to—"

Cyrus grabbed my arm and spun me around, "No Shawn, look at that kid. He's going to get stuck."

And just then, the young boy who'd been playing at the skee-ball machine screamed a bloodcurdling scream. He'd stuck his hand into the ball dispenser and gotten it caught. His mother yelled for help and suddenly everything around us started moving in slow motion. She cried and pulled out her phone. People stopped and stared. I looked back at the team to see if anyone was going to do something.

But Cyrus did not get caught up in the moment. He swiftly uncapped the tools in his fingertips and started taking off the cover of the ball dispenser. The screwdriver in his pinkie helped him get the heavy, metal cover off. Once he was inside the machine, he used the scissors in his thumb to snip the boy's shirt that had caught on a bolt.

"You have a broken bone in your wrist, and a few scrapes, but you'll be fine," Cyrus said calmly as the little boy watched him in amazement. The boy was still crying, but he was free.

"What were you thinking?" the boy's mother cried helplessly as she hugged her son.

The boy frowned. "The machine cheated me out of a ball. I was going to get it myself."

The mom wiped her tears away and looked up at Cyrus. "Thank you so much. You're a hero!"

Cyrus looked a little flustered. He glanced at me and said, "Shawn, look in that first aid kit and find the antibacterial ointment and gauze wrap."

In the commotion, I hadn't even noticed that one of the waitresses had brought out the first aid kit. I tossed the tube of ointment and gauze to Cyrus, who had the boy all wrapped up before the ambulance and fire truck arrived. Once everyone in the restaurant recovered from the shock of what had just happened, they started chanting, "Cy-rus, Cy-rus, Cy-rus!"

I looked over at the team. Demarcus waved me

over to show me that he'd made a video of the whole incident. I knew what I had promised Cyrus, but we had to share this experience with everyone else.

"Send it," I whispered, and hoped I wouldn't regret it.

———

When I woke up the next morning, I rolled over in bed and looked at my phone. The video had gone viral overnight. Cyrus was an international hero. I grinned and jumped out of bed.

"Mom!" I hollered as I ran down the stairs. "Guess what! Oh—" My parents and Cyrus were sitting in the living room with Dr. Smith. I looked down at my dinosaur pajama bottoms and thought about running back upstairs, but my mom smiled and patted the couch cushion next to her.

When I sat down, Dr. Smith spoke. "So you are responsible for the video?"

I hung my head. "Yes, sir. I know you thought they were silly, but—"

"But nothing, son. This video is exactly what we want people to see. Cyrus stayed cool and collected and stepped into action, which is more than we can say for the humans in the restaurant. This is the kind of media attention that moves our vision forward. Well done!"

I looked up and smiled. "So, Cyrus can stay?"

"Thanks to you," my dad said, looking over at me.

"And he's going to keep living here and Dr. Geno won't bother us anymore?" I asked.

"Actually, we're working on that. How would you feel if we made Cyrus our personal property, by adopting him?" my mom asked with a smile.

"You can do that?" I was surprised but excited by the idea of Cyrus being around for good.

My dad smiled. "We're working on it."

"What do you think, Cyrus?" I asked, looking over at the world's latest hero.

"I think this family is always looking out for each other and I want nothing more than to stay," Cyrus said confidently.

"Well then," Dr. Smith said as he stood up. "It's settled. CY-159, you will officially become Cyrus Cole."

We all liked that sound of that.